D0353201

FREE
RAPTORS
4 903684 000

For Birdie,
and all the other raptors
I've known

First published 2014 by Walker Books Ltd
87 Vauxhall Walk, London SE11 5HJ

2 4 6 8 10 9 7 5 3 1

This book has been typeset in Aunt Mildred

Printed in China

British Library Cataloguing in Publication Data:
a catalogue record for this book is available from the British Library

ISBN 978-1-4063-5662-5

www.walker.co.uk

If I Had a Velociraptor

George O'Connor

WALKER BOOKS
AND SUBSIDIARIES
LONDON • BOSTON • SYDNEY • AUCKLAND

If I had a velociraptor,
I'd want to get her as a baby,
when she's all teensy and tiny
and funny and fluffy.

A baby raptor is so teensy and tiny

that she would be easy to lose.

I'd give her a little bell

so I could always find her.

Ring-a-ding-ding!
There you are!

Baby raptors are the cutest!

If I had a velociraptor,
she would like to sit on my lap,
and I would let her.

Even when she grew up,
she would still like to sit on my lap.

A raptor likes nothing better
than a nice warm spot.
My raptor would bask on
a sunny windowsill

or snuggle in the
clean laundry.

She would even settle on my homework.
Or in any cosy little space, really.

My raptor would like to sleep.

She would sleep a LOT.

She would sleep all day long.

Because she would probably
definitely run around like crazy.

She would run around like crazy

all

night

long.

Raptors have special eyes
that let them see in the dark.

(I don't.)

No matter how late she stayed up,
my raptor would wake me up nice and early.

She would let me know when
she was hungry.

Or not.

If I had a velociraptor,
I would have to
teach her what's right
and what's wrong.

I might even have to
trim her claws a little bit
now and then.

She would always
forgive me, though.
Good girl!

All raptors like to hunt.
If I had a velociraptor,
she would stalk the little things
that catch her eye, like birds,
or insects, or even a dust bunny.

Sometimes she would
stare at nothing at all or
at I wouldn't even know what.

And sometimes
she might just stare at me.

If I had a velociraptor…

There you are!

it would be the best thing ever.